THE INVINCIBLE KINGDOM

Crocodile Books, USA

An imprint of Interlink Publishing Group, Inc.

www.interlinkbooks.com

S OMETIMES IT SEEMS AS if everything is going along just fine. We find ourselves settled and contented; things seem to be better than they have ever been before; we feel we are in the place we want to be and, better still, heading in the direction we want to be going.

But then, from out of nowhere, a giant mountain is suddenly placed in our path, and since there is no way to get around it, all we can do is stride forward determinedly.

The journey becomes steeper and more exhausting with every step, yet the summit of the mountain never seems to get any closer. All we can do is keep on climbing.

A NOT DISSIMILAR SITUATION CONFRONTED the hero of our story.

Born into the Royal family, he was the rightful heir to the throne and when his father died he had become King, a life that in his heart he had never once desired. Having escaped to the world beyond the palace walls, he endeavored to forge a new future for himself.

No-one knew who he really was. He made new friends, found work, and even a place to call home; and more importantly, he met somebody he wanted to love.

After a precious evening sharing secrets, John and June strolled happily through the park. John had received an unusual message from the Palace Bootman, his sole friend from his old life as King, urging him to meet by the statue of the Giant Cat at eleven o'clock that morning.

June watched her friend walk away towards his mysterious assignation with an uneasy feeling. *Something's not quite right*, she thought to herself, and turned around and began to follow him.

It was a sunny day and the park was already busy; a group of boys played a game of cricket while people strolled around, rode bicycle, and did all the normal things people do on a fine morning. But in the distance, June could see John and the person she guessed was his friend, surrounded by several threatening-looking men.

June began to run.

SEEING THAT JOHN WAS in trouble, June acted quickly. At school she had been captain of the cricket team, and now she grabbed a bat from the hands of a boy and yelled at the bowler to bowl as fast as he could. She swung the bat back and struck the ball harder than she had ever hit anything in her life.

The ball rocketed through the air until it collided with a resounding THUD with the back of John's head. His legs buckled and he fell to the ground.

The frozen silence that follows a horrible accident was followed by a gasp of shock as people all around rushed to help.

"Let me through; I'm a doctor!" called out a man in a hat as he took charge of the situation.

"Somebody call an ambulance," he said as he knelt down beside John, who was knocked out cold.

June pushed her way through the crowd that had quickly gathered.

"I'm his girlfriend! Is he all right?"

As she knelt beside him, taking his hand in hers, she glanced around. The mysterious men had vanished into thin air.

I N ALMOST NO TIME at all,
an ambulance arrived at the scene and John,
still unconscious and with June by his side, was stretchered
through the inquisitive crowd.

As the ambulance raced through the city streets, lights flashing and sirens wailing,
June sat beside her friend, trying to work out what had just happened.

"Ooh, my head hurts," groaned a small voice beside her.

"Oh, thank heavens you're all right!" June gasped with relief as John tried to sit up.

But as they drew up to the hospital, June could see that there were several armed
guards waiting at the gates, and she was sure that she spotted some of the men from
the park among them.

"Seeing as he's now conscious," June asked the paramedic, "is there any place you
could pull over and let us out?"

"No can do, miss. We have to take you all the way to the hospital." And he called out
to the driver for confirmation of this fact: "That's the rules, isn't it, Fred?"

A kind pair of eyes looked back at them in the rear-view mirror. "That's right, George,
such as it is, even though we have a celebrity on board."

June and John stared at each other in horror, panicking that he must have been
recognized as the King.

"Yes, indeed," continued the driver. "When I was down on my luck a while back this
young lady right here used to give out food to needy folk like me, she was famous for
her kindness. Of course you won't remember me, but night after night you filled my

belly not only with hot food but with kind words and a friendly smile. You're a saint as far as I'm concerned, miss."

June blushed, and then pleaded with the two ambulance men: "We really need help, those men outside are after us—please don't stop here!"

"I'll tell you what, miss, the rules say we have to take you to the hospital, but they don't say exactly where. What if we drop you off all the way around the back?"

The ambulance sped past the armed guards before coming to a stop on the opposite side of the hospital.

"Thank you!" John and June exclaimed as they climbed out.

"One good turn deserves another, miss!" the driver said in return as they hurried away down the empty street.

WITHOUT EXCHANGING A SINGLE word, John and June walked as quickly as they could through the city.

After twenty minutes or so they found themselves in an area famous for its vast museums.

As their frantic pace began to slow down, June whispered in her friend's ear, "We will be safer among the crowds in here," and she steered him into the cavernous entrance hall of the Museum of Natural History.

After finding a quiet corner in the Great Hall of Dinosaurs, June told John that it was she who had knocked him out with a cricket ball. "And now," she said, "you need to tell me all about those men who were trying to kidnap you, and why there were armed guards waiting to arrest you at the hospital."

John explained that Lord Von Dronus, his former guardian, had never forgiven him for running away; and that Von Dronus had pretended the King was gravely ill and installed a fake king in his place. But now Von Dronus knew that John was alive, he had to make sure that John couldn't expose the cover-up and, as Von Dronus had whispered menacingly in John's ear just a few hours ago, the only way to ensure his secret was safe was to make John disappear for good.

"Oh my goodness, Von Dronus won't give up now! He will have his spies hunting everywhere for you!" June exclaimed, the panic rising in her voice.

All that afternoon they discussed what they should do next, and as they did they realized how few options they had.

"Please don't worry," John said, smiling at her reassuringly. "I know dozens of places all over the city where we can go to ground. Look at the bones of these giant creatures that walked this same planet as us. All they were concerned about was surviving. There was always some other even bigger dinosaur trying to eat them up, so just making it to the end of each day was enough for them. That is what we need to do."

THEY LEFT THE MUSEUM and weaved their way down alleyways and side streets until they came to a narrow church squeezed between two buildings so tightly you hardly even noticed it was there.

Inside, all was dark and quiet and John led June past the empty rows of pews to a low door set into a thick wall at the rear of the chapel.

"This door is kept locked, but when I had no place to live I used to sit in this church for hours to keep out of the rain, and I noticed that the verger used to hide the key …" He reached up to a ledge above the door frame. "Right here!" he exclaimed triumphantly.

The door led into the bell tower, which was made up of a series of small rooms piled one on top of the other, all of them empty except for the ropes that ran through the rooms from floor to ceiling, all the way to the belfry at the very top.

"No one will ever find us up here. We can rest in safety, at least for tonight."

And although it was not late, as the room gradually got darker their talking ceased and it was not long before they both fell fast asleep on the dusty floorboards.

The following morning they woke hungry and aching all over.

"Come upstairs and get some fresh air," John called out to June as he climbed the ladder to the belfry above them.

A narrow balcony ran around the outside of the tower and the two of them inhaled the fresh morning air as if it were a meal in itself.

"How peaceful it looks down there," June said, sighing. "You would hardly believe that anyone had any worries or troubles in their lives from way up here."

John frowned. "I wish I knew someone I could ask for help, but I'd rather hand myself in at the palace gate than get anyone into trouble on my account."

June nodded as she gazed towards the west of the city, far away on the other side of the river. "There is one person that I could ask," she said. "We would have to leave straight away if we are to catch him before he leaves for work."

As they stepped on to the street, rush hour was just beginning. The fugitives were aware that any of the countless people they passed could be one of Von Dronus's spies.

O NCE THEY HAD CROSSED over the bridge spanning the river that divided the city in two, the streets were no longer full of shops and offices, and became much quieter and more residential.

On an affluent-looking, tree-lined avenue, June stopped abruptly outside a bright red door belonging to a bright pink house.

As she lifted the heavy brass knocker, June paused and turned to John. "This house belongs to a man that once made me a promise. He vowed that if I ever needed help in any way he would always be there. Oh well," she said ruefully as she let the knocker drop, "let's see if he's as good as his word."

A few seconds later a smartly dressed, bespectacled man opened the door and his face switched to an expression of pure delight as he recognized his visitor.

"June!"

T HIS LAUGHING MAN SWEPT
June up in his arms and gave her the
biggest ever hug!

"Come in, come in," he urged them both. "You're
visiting early, I must say! Five minutes later and I'd have left for
work and missed you!"

June took her old friend's hand in hers. "Brian, do you remember that you once
said I could always ask you for help? Well, today I am asking."

On hearing these words, Brian's naturally cheerful countenance changed and he
became much more somber as he looked at the two of them intently.

"As long as you both promise to be here when I return, then I'm sure that there's
nothing so serious that we can't sort it out together this evening."

He quickly showed them about the house, urging them to make themselves
comfortable and to be sure to help themselves to anything and everything they
needed. And then he was gone.

But that evening, when Brian returned home, his face looked pale and worried.

"Did anyone come to the door? Did you leave the house? Was everything OK?
Are you safe?" he asked them.

When they assured him that all had been quiet, he breathed a sigh of relief. He told
them that on the way home from work he had seen hundreds of "Wanted" posters
plastered across the city walls, declaring them enemies of the Kingdom.

"BEFORE EITHER OF YOU utter a single word," Brian said to them, raising his hand in the air, "I am going to prepare us a nourishing and hopefully delicious meal and when it is ready we three shall sit down and you can tell me what is going on."

And as he opened the kitchen door he looked back and smiled at the two of them reassuringly.

"Whatever you tell me and whatever has happened, we will work it out."

Dinner that night was very long as they told Brian every single detail of John's incredible story. They told him about his life as a "boy" prince and how, when his father died, he had become King. They told him about the way he used to escape from the palace at night and how he had explored the city as if he were a free man, and how he had realized that Lord Von Dronus suspected what he was up to, and that made him decide to leave the palace and never return.

Brian learned how the young man had struggled to survive all alone in the world, how he'd been homeless, and how he had met June at her food kitchen and begun helping her before getting a job in Angelo and Theresa's café, and finally how John and June had become friends. All of which had led to the fateful meeting with the Bootman, being pounced upon by Von Dronus and his henchmen, fleeing the ambulance, and hiding in museums and churches, right up to this very morning when they had knocked on his door.

They told him every single thing, and when they had finished Brian considered them intently for a long time before he spoke.

"You have both behaved impeccably. But there is no doubt, as we say in court, that you are both in a very compromising situation. The palace has announced that tonight there will be a special emergency broadcast on television. Might I suggest that we retire to the parlor to see what Von Dronus's next move will be?"

Lord Von Dronus's angry face almost filled the entire screen. "Loyal subjects of our beloved nation," he began, "I have some very distressing news to impart to you this evening. Thanks to the tireless watchfulness of our security services, a secret plot has been uncovered.

"Dangerous enemies of our country intended to endanger the life of our beloved monarch. Thankfully this outrageous plot has been foiled, but unfortunately the evil perpetrators that intended to commit this foul deed are still at large somewhere in our country. It is probable that they are still in the capital. Please, I urge you, do not approach these dangerous people. Instead immediately call for the police."

At this point Lord Von Dronus paused and leaned in even closer to the camera. It was almost as if he was trying to reach out and speak directly to John. As he lowered his voice, Von Dronus's words took on an even more menacing tone: "Our beloved Royal family is the one thing that remains unchanged in an ever-changing world. The King represents stability and order and now some irresponsible people wish to eradicate this.

"I have this to say to these revolutionaries: You will not be allowed to change things from the way they are. You will not change all that we believe in and all that we stand for and I urge every loyal subject to help hunt you down. We will find you. You will be stopped, in the name of the King!"

The sound of the National Anthem came in as the Lord's face faded from the screen.

BRIAN REACHED OVER AND turned the television set off.

"Well, one good thing came out of that!" he exclaimed with a smile. "I now realize that the man is a complete idiot." And he burst out laughing.

"All this talk about resisting change … does he not realize that our entire universe is ruled by change?" He shook his head in disbelief. "Poor Lord Von Dronus, he couldn't have got it more wrong.

"All around us the world is changing every single second, from the tiniest atom to the hugest star! Our bodies change food into energy, the seasons change, the universe is ever expanding. The laws of nature are governed by change and to go against it is to set yourself against nature itself!"

Jumping up from his armchair, he raised his hands high above his head.

"Reach up with me!" he shouted to June and John. "Reach up and feel the constantly changing atoms that are all around us. Reach up and try to imagine them buzzing and spinning all around us—come on," he urged, "come and feel this vibrant universe we live in!"

And John and June leapt up and all three of them danced around together, their arms waving in the air. They knew at that moment that Lord Von Dronus was wrong and they were right.

Laughing together, they slumped back in their chairs. Brian sighed and looked across at June. "Do you remember when we first met?" And for someone usually so full of the joys of life, he now looked quite forlorn.

"It was not long after Mother had died. I had lost all interest in the world, in everything. I was lost. All I was able to do was restlessly walk the streets all day and all night, until the evening when I met you and your little van freely giving food to people simply because they needed it. Do you remember what you said to me?"

June smiled shyly and nodded.

"You took my hands in yours," Brian continued, "and you said to me, 'I know that it feels as if everything inside you has broken into tiny fragments, and I know you think that it's beyond even attempting to fix, but I know that one tiny piece at a time we can glue it back together. I can help you do it if that's what you'd like.' June, you saved my life that night and I have never forgotten it."

And then Brian stood up and he took their hands in his as he looked into their eyes and solemnly proclaimed, "I make this promise to both of you: that I will protect and help you in any way that I can. I will never break this promise."

BRIAN INSISTED THAT THEY had no option but to stay with him. Perhaps some time in the future their lives might return to the way they were, but for the time being they would be safest hiding in his house.

And so their lives in exile began. At first their days lacked any order. They would wake up at any hour that suited them and drift aimlessly about the house. They would spend hours looking out of the windows, enviously watching the world carrying on as normal, indifferent to whether they were a part of it or not.

Climbing out of bed one afternoon, June announced, "We need structure in our lives." And she began to write a detailed itinerary for

them to follow.
They would,
from now on,
wake early,
prepare Brian's
breakfast, have
a disco-dancing
session, spend an
hour reading to each
other, an hour listening
to music, an hour cleaning
the house, watch their favorite
afternoon quiz show on television, knit
and draw, write their diaries, prepare
dinner for Brian, write poetry, and so
on, and so on.

It seemed that the more they tried to fit
into their days, the happier they became.

It really wasn't such a bad life. When
you meet somebody you
want to love, you want
to be with that person
every single hour of
every day. You want
to build a world
around yourselves,
and this is just what
John and June did.

SOME PEOPLE LIVE IN the past, believing that their best years are behind them; most people live in the present, looking forward only as far as the next weekend or their holidays; but John and June, whose present was on hold, created a world of their own. They daydreamed about all the things they would make happen when they could venture outside again.

They discovered they shared a love of drawing. One of their favorite projects was designing the layouts for houses that they would like to live in, and they amassed hundreds of these fantastical plans.

One day John decided he was going to direct a film, but without a camera or actors he had to imagine all of it in his head. He drew every single scene and, every night, he would tell an enraptured June the latest twists and turns in the complex plot.

John's other great artistic passion was drawing picture after picture of the sea. When June finally asked him why he always drew the same thing, he answered, "I've never been to the seaside. It's my dream to visit it and maybe even go in it—how wonderful that would be!"

As THE WEEKS WENT by, there seemed to be no let-up in Von Dronus's campaign.

But Brian always assured his two young visitors that they were welcome to stay with him as long as they wanted to or had to. In fact he readily declared that he enjoyed the pleasure of their company, and always ended this little speech by saying dramatically, "One day you will both be gone and I will be left alone here, heartbroken."

But as time passed, there was one thing that lowered the morale of the two young fugitives. They would sit looking out of the round window in the highest room of the house, longing for the simple pleasure of going for a walk, wishing they could be outside in the fresh air.

On wet and windy
days, June in
particular would
fret and worry about
how all the people
she had fed from her
little van would be
faring without her, and
on the darkest, coldest
days John could hear her
mutter quietly to herself,
"They must all think that
I have abandoned them."

She tried to hide it from him,
but John knew she was crying
to herself.

All this mess is my fault, he thought in
his darkest moods. *I'm ruining June's life
and I'm putting Brian in danger and it's all
my selfish fault.*

As he lay there in the middle of the night trying
to think of a way out of their desperate situation,
he could only ever come up with one solution.
To hand himself over to Lord Von Dronus.

THE FOLLOWING MORNING, JOHN told June that he had been thinking. "I'm really sorry about the way things have worked out," he said. "I never dreamed that Von Dronus would go after me so relentlessly. I really believed that once he had replaced me with a doppelgänger I would be off the hook … And I hate seeing you cooped up in here," he added.

"But I really don't mind," June tried to argue back at him.

"Please, June, just hear me out. I escaped from the palace because I felt like a prisoner in there, but now I feel like a prisoner in here. Nothing has changed except that I've managed to imprison you as well, and it's more than I can bear!" John sobbed.

He took her hand as a tear rolled down his cheek. "I know you will tell me not to, but I have decided to hand myself over to Von Dronus."

June gently pressed her finger against his lips. "Now it's your turn to listen to me," she softly whispered.

"A thousand years of kings reigned in line before you, but not one of them was brave enough to actually go through with what you did—though I'm sure many dreamed of it. You were the only one who dared to change your life! And never mind the fact you were a king. Out of the tens of thousands of teenage boys who live in this city, only one of them climbed out of their bedroom window at night to roam the streets all alone, just because they were compelled by an urge they could not suppress to explore the silent poetry of the sleeping city.

"But YOU did. Only YOU. And why?" She smiled as she asked this question. "Because you are special. You are different and you dared to dream different dreams. All of my life I have wanted to meet somebody with whom I could share the real me, and that night when you asked me to come to yours for dinner I knew that my days of being alone were finally over, so there is no way that I'm going to sit here and let you go so easily!

"Look, in two days' time it is your birthday. I'll make a deal with you: stay with me until then, because I've got you a really special present, and after I have given it to you then you are free to go and I won't try to stop you. Is it a deal?"

John nodded reluctantly. "OK, I'll stay. Just until my birthday."

A COUPLE OF DAYS LATER, John awoke to see June sitting at the end of his bed.

"Happy birthday!" she shouted excitedly. "Get dressed quickly, birthday boy, because I can't give you your present here, I have to take you to it."

Covering his eyes with her hands, she led him down the stairs to the garage at the rear of the house.

"Surprise!" she yelled out as she pulled her hands away. Standing right before him was a shiny red motor scooter!

"Brian arranged it all!" June exclaimed, almost bursting with excitement.

"It's very nice," John said hesitantly, not wishing to dampen June's enthusiasm, "but it's not like we're free to go outside for a ride. What are we going to do? Ride it around in circles inside this garage?"

"But check this out," June replied as she reached down and pulled up a pair of crash helmets complete with big motorcyclist's goggles.

"Imagine us wearing these, with scarves covering the rest of our faces! We can whizz around, completely unrecognized! We can ride out to the countryside, and once we're somewhere quiet with no one about we can take them off!"

John burst out laughing, and as he realized what she was saying he grabbed June and hugged her. "You are the greatest genius that ever lived!"

The doors of the garage led to a narrow alley that fed into a side street running behind the house. It was backed by a high brick wall that kept it totally hidden from the rears of the neighboring houses. No one would ever see them coming or going.

"Where are we going to go?" shouted John, trying to make himself heard above the sound of the engine and clinging on to June's waist as they drove down the alleyway.

"I can't tell you," she called back, "it's a surprise!"

As they made their way through the streets, they felt a sense of elation to be finally back in the outside world again. Through their tinted goggles they stared in wonder at the crowds of people, but not a single person gave John or June so much as a glance.

It was as if they had become totally invisible in their new disguises. But if anyone could see beneath John and June's scarves, they would see that they were grinning from ear to ear!

THEY RODE THROUGH THE city streets and the houses became smaller and further apart until they soon found themselves surrounded by green fields, and as they lowered their scarves a delicious bouquet of grass and flowers and hay greeted their noses. Finding an isolated place to park, they warily removed their goggles and helmets.

"I've got something I want to show you," June said, and she led the way up the sandy path of a small hill. When they reached the top, there, stretching out before them, as far as they could see, was the ocean.

"Happy birthday, darling," June said as she kissed John on the cheek.

They sat on the sand dunes eating the packed lunch June had brought, and when they had finished June pulled towels and swimsuits from the bottom of her bag.

The water was freezing cold at first, but June insisted that if they rushed in up to their necks all at once then it wouldn't be so bad, and it wasn't.

When they got home at the end of that long day they were both completely exhausted.

"Well," said June triumphantly, "do you still want to go back to the palace or would you rather stay here with me, where every day could be an adventure?"

"The latter," John said as he sat and remembered the feeling of the sea flowing around him.

WITH THE ARRIVAL OF the motor scooter, their days changed beyond all recognition.

On their next excursion they rode out deep into the countryside and parked on the edge of a great wood. They walked and walked, and June showed John the many different types of wild flowers her mother had shown her when she was a little girl.

"When I was young," John recalled, "elaborate arrangements of flowers in huge vases appeared every morning as if by magic. Each bloom was specially chosen for its beauty by the greatest florists in the land. But none," said John, examining a tiny white daisy, "was as beautiful as this."

ON ANOTHER DAY, JOHN and June rode out of the city further than they had ever gone before, to a part of the country full of valleys and rolling hills.

After a very long and very steep walk they stood exhausted at the top of a hill, feeling their hearts pound as the wind whistled wildly around them.

Pointing up towards a pair of birds soaring overhead, John asked his friend, "If you could have a superpower, what would it be?"

"What do you mean, 'if'?" June laughed. "I've already got a superpower!"

"Is it a secret or am I allowed to know?"

"Well, only as long as you keep it to yourself," she replied, and then quite suddenly she became serious and the silence that you only get at the top of a mountain seemed to wrap itself around them. "I am able to see the loneliness in people's hearts and make them feel less lonely," she said.

John thought quietly for a while before replying, "Yes, I think I already knew that."

"And yours," she said excitedly, "is that you can take a plain piece of paper and a pencil and create a whole new world. You can draw the places you want to go and the people you want to meet. With some paper and your imagination you can tell a thousand stories. That's your superpower— you're an artist!"

THAT EVENING, AS THEY returned from a blissful day, they noticed that in almost every street, groups of policemen appeared to be stopping people at random. Be they elderly pensioners or young married couples, they were being pulled aside and asked to produce identification, which was then thoroughly scrutinized.

Over dinner at the Pink House, John asked Brian if he knew what was going on. With a sigh, Brian confessed that these spot checks had been happening for several days and that that wasn't the only bad news. Then he opened the newspaper and they saw the articles detailing how the search for John and June would continue. A map illustrated how the city would be split up into areas where, in due course, every house and every building would be systematically searched.

As June and John sat on either side of their protector, trying to absorb these new developments, they said nothing. Brian smiled at them both, but they could see that he was putting on a brave face for their benefit.

"Yes, I know it looks bad, but all is not yet lost," he said. "I will start arranging a plan to smuggle you out of the country." His voice was full of anxiety as he added, "I just need more time. This is all my fault." Brian reached out and wrapped his strong arms around them both. "I promised to protect you—and I have failed. I should have got you away to safety a long time ago, to a place as far away from the palace as possible."

As Brian tried to hide his feelings of despair, little did he realize that his words had planted a small seed of an idea in John's mind.

L ATER THAT NIGHT, WAY
past midnight, June was woken
by John. He was dressed all
in black, with a hooded top
covering his head.

"What are you doing? Are you handing
yourself over to the palace?"

"Don't worry, I'll be back in a few hours,"
John answered evasively.

"So will I," she said as she climbed out of bed
and began getting dressed, "because I'm coming with you."

"Wear something dark—black if possible. We can't afford to be seen," John said,
pretending to be a bit annoyed. Deep down, he was relieved that after all they'd
been through they would not be separated on this most crucial night. Soon June
was ready and they slipped out of the back of the house into the cool night air.

They stayed well away from the main roads, sticking to back streets and even
smaller and darker alleyways. Occasionally a lone car or person would appear
ahead or behind them and they would disappear down passageways or hide in
doorways, becoming invisible in the shadows they afforded.

"Are we anywhere near wherever it is we're going?" June asked after a long time.

Coming to a stop, John replied, "We're very close now. Follow me." He pulled himself up over a low wall. On the other side was a grassy embankment sloping down to a lone railway track, which led into a pitch-black tunnel.

Either side of the tunnel's opening were signs that warned you not to enter, promising extreme danger and prosecution to anyone who dared to disobey. June looked at the signs and then at John with an expression that said, *Are you quite sure you know what you're doing?*

"No trains will come in or out of here, not at this time. I promise those signs are there mainly to scare people away. Besides, I'm not trespassing: technically all of this land, including this tunnel, belongs to me."

"Well, the signs worked—I'm scared," June said, "but I'm still going with you."

"Brilliant," he said, and he grasped her hand and led the way into the intense blackness.

IT WAS SO DARK inside the tunnel
that the beam from John's torch only illuminated a few feet ahead.
The walls were lined with dusty soot, and oily water dripped down them,
gathering in large greasy puddles that they had to leap across. Occasionally
they heard scratching sounds ahead of them, which they guessed
were rats. Steadily, the two of them walked along the
railway track, stepping carefully from
beam to beam.

For about an hour they trudged on
as the tunnel twisted and turned. But soon they saw a soft glow far
ahead in the distance, and as they walked gratefully towards it, it got
ever brighter until they turned a final bend. There before them, in utter
contrast to the dingy tunnel, was a station platform—
but one unlike any June had ever seen!

The platform
itself was luxuriously carpeted,
and the soft yellow light came from a series of sparkling crystal
chandeliers hanging from the roof of the tunnel.

"Now, if my memory serves me right," John said as he
pushed down on a crown set into the ornate paneled
walls, "this should open the door." A click sounded
as a secret panel sprang open.

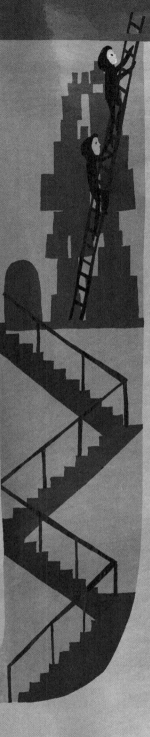

June could hold back her astonishment no longer. "Where on earth are we?"

In fact they were far below the Royal palace, lower than the deepest basement. The ornate platform was part of an old secret railway that the Royal family had used when they needed to travel to other parts of the Kingdom. Though it was used so rarely that most people in the palace had forgotten it existed, when John was young he had traveled on the train many times and, being an inquisitive boy, he had noticed the spot where the train exited the tunnel from the palace. *You never know when such information might come in useful*, he had thought at the time.

The secret door on the platform led to yet another dimly lit passage and eventually to a tall staircase.

"We're nearly there," John called back to June. He moved purposefully now, as if each stone was familiar to him, which of course it was.

As they finally climbed the last step, John pushed open a tiny trapdoor in the ceiling and they climbed into a long dark corridor, at the far end of which John stopped and opened yet another trapdoor.

"Jump after me. Don't worry, it's a soft landing!" he said as he dropped through the hole in the floor.

H E LANDED ON TOP of a giant four-poster bed. As John lowered himself down gently he saw that the man beneath the covers was still fast asleep. Glad that he had not woken him, John could not resist looking at this mysterious stranger, the man the entire nation believed was their King.

Although this man had a beard, he and John could still almost be taken for identical twins, and as John peered at his face, he saw for the first time what he looked like when he was asleep. It was a unique sensation.

Where did Von Dronus find this man? John thought to himself. *And who is he?*

Just as he was trying to work out the gentlest way to wake the sleeping man, June fell through the trapdoor and landed with a heavy thud.

Startled, the bearded man sat bolt upright and began to call out, "Help! Guards! Assassins!!"

John and June rushed forward and grabbed hold of him, covering his mouth with their hands as he struggled to get away from them.

"Shush, shush, please!" John whispered imploringly, knowing that a pair of palace guards would be standing watch outside the bedroom door.

"We're not here to hurt you!" he pleaded. "It's hard for you to believe, but this was once my bed. I am the real King, the King that you replaced!"

The man in the bed stopped struggling, staring at them in astonishment.

"If I remove my hand and let go of you," John reasoned, "will you give me one minute to prove who I am? Then, if you don't believe me, you can go ahead and call the guards."

The fake King nodded.

They released him and John quickly began to tell the story of how, when he was the young Prince, he used to lie in this same bed, drawing an imaginary town on the drapes that now surrounded them. "How would anyone but me, the real King, know that secret?" John asked.

"But there's nothing there—there's no proof at all," the man replied, pointing up at the plain curtains.

"But look now." John pressed a special switch on his flashlight and, as if by magic, finely inked drawings appeared all over the fabric, glowing in the dark.

T HE MAN IN THE bed stared at John in amazement. "But you're not dead?"

John and June looked at him curiously.

"No! Why would you think that?" John replied, slightly indignantly. "I didn't die, I just ran away."

"Then everything I have been told is a lie."

And now the pretend King told his story. His name was Terry and he had been a soldier in the army when Lord Von Dronus began to pay special attention to him. One day he was sent on a special mission to guard a lonely lighthouse set high up on a cliff, miles from anywhere.

"It was so tedious, staring at the sea all day. My only command was to grow a beard, but being the good soldier I was I never questioned the orders given to me, no matter how peculiar they seemed. Then, out of the blue one night, Von Dronus appeared at the lighthouse, alone." He told Terry how the King had been murdered, poisoned by enemies of their country. Von Dronus explained how he had managed to keep it a secret from everybody by announcing that the King had contracted a contagious illness. It was a matter of the utmost importance to the nation's security that nobody ever knew what had really happened, as it could destabilize the whole country. Lord Von Dronus said that due to Terry's uncanny physical resemblance to the King, he had been chosen to secretly take his place. The nation would be told that the King had recovered, and nobody would ever know he had been murdered.

"And ever since then, it's been little old me on the throne," laughed the fake King. "I'll tell you what, though," he added, "it isn't half boring!"

"Tell me about it!" John said, laughing too.

John said that he had a plan that might just help them both be the people they really wanted to be. It was quite complex and took a while to explain, but when he had finally finished Terry said with a big smile all over his face, "It's so crazy it might just work!"

THE FOLLOWING EVENING, BRIAN, John and June sat down to watch a classical music concert on television. It was a special performance and as such the King was in attendance, but just before it was about to start the King (or should I say Terry) got up from his seat and loudly asked if he could have a go. Not quite knowing what to do, the conductor handed over his baton—after all, in a thousand years nobody had ever said no to a monarch before.

The music sounded awful as the orchestra attempted to keep time with the King's manically waving arm. At first the audience laughed, thinking it was a planned joke, but the laughter faded as the King continued to conduct the entire symphony, all two hours of it.

Brian looked over to John and June. "Well, I've never seen the like!" he exclaimed, but he didn't see the two friends smile and secretly wink to each other.

At the Soccer Cup Final the following Saturday afternoon, more unusual Royal behavior occurred when the King walked down from the Royal box on to the field and demanded to be allowed to play.

The referee, quickly trying to stop this travesty, exclaimed, "But, Your Majesty, you have no cleats!"

"That's no problem!" he shouted as he slipped off his shoes. "I'll play barefoot!"

Of course, none of the other players dared to tackle the King and he ended up scoring three goals, which he celebrated extravagantly. There were several boos from the crowd, and even before the final whistle the stadium was half empty.

At the end of the match there was the unusual spectacle of the monarch presenting the winner's cup to himself.

Later that evening, as he relaxed in his bedroom, Terry the fake King received a visit from Lord Von Dronus.

"I don't know what you are playing at, but this ridiculous behavior has got to stop immediately," the Lord hissed menacingly.

"I thought it added a touch of realism to my role," Terry replied cheerfully. "I thought kings behaved however they wanted."

Von Dronus exploded with anger. "You're no king!" he shouted furiously.

"Don't ever forget," he threatened, "I can make you disappear just as quickly as you appeared. From now on, all your Royal appearances will be canceled—you won't have any more opportunities to embarrass us ever again." And he stormed out of the room.

But for all the power he wielded, there were still some events in the country's calendar that Lord Von Dronus had no control over. The coming Sunday was the day when the nation honored their countrymen who had perished in times of war. It was called "Heroes Day" and the King would simply have to be present.

The ceremony was always televised, and John and June could not believe their eyes when they saw cameras zooming in on the Royal podium. Instead of gravely saluting the ranks of soldiers marching by, the King was reading a comic book and laughing to himself.

"The Lord won't be happy when he sees this," June commented gleefully, to which John added, "The whole country won't be too happy either!"

I NDEED THEY WERE NOT. There was national outrage!

The people were already shocked at the King's recent behavior, but this latest disrespectful show was truly beyond the pale. In the newspapers and on the television the public aired their opinions on the King's disgraceful behavior, and the verdict was unanimous: he had acted abominably.

Meanwhile, in the palace, Lord Von Dronus was practically pulling his hair out in frustration as he screamed at Terry.

"I have arranged a special press conference and you will profusely apologize to everybody. You will say what is written in front of you, nothing else! Do you understand?"

At the press conference Terry did apologize to the nation, sincerely and genuinely. He read out the message that Lord Von Dronus had prepared, but then continued with an announcement of his own.

"I believe that the underlying reason for my disrespectful behavior of late is because deep down I am lonely. What I need is someone with whom I can settle down. I truly believe that my Queen, whoever she may be, will tame these wild and impetuous urges that seize me, and it is my most serious intent to begin my search for her immediately."

The King's
apology met with
a rather lukewarm reception from
the populace, but it did at least please one person.

Lord Von Dronus was sure that if he could find a young, impressionable
girl willing to marry the wayward King, then he could manipulate her and help
control Terry. Perhaps she could become the Royal figurehead—after all, people always
loved a real princess. That way, he would be free to get rid of the fake King and let her
rule as Queen.

The Lord arranged a series of balls at the palace to which he had invited many eligible
young ladies, but the King showed little interest in any of them.

Then, one night, there appeared at
the palace a very striking woman in
a costume that resembled a lizard,
accompanied by two lizards on
golden chains. She was none other
than the world-famous avant-
garde fashion designer Countess
Forbici.

And after just one look at
her, the King was completely
and absolutely smitten.

A ND THUS BEGAN THE most bizarre Royal romance that the Kingdom had ever seen. The King was besotted and the two of them became inseparable.

Much to the horror of Lord Von Dronus, the King insisted that she design him an entirely new wardrobe, a commission that she took on with great relish. Before long the two of them were creating quite a stir among the city's fashion elite.

Countess Forbici's ambition to restyle the monarchy did not end with merely dressing the King: before long she was working on a new and radical look for the palace guardsmen.

"We need a much stronger silhouette, bigger shapes, bolder colors. Everything in this palace is so drab," she announced, much to the anger of Lord Von Dronus. But it did not end there.

One day Countess Forbici declared that she was going to redesign the nation's flag.

"The country needs something less old-fashioned and more dynamic. The new design will be a glorious explosion of neon colors!"

All of these dramatic changes happened over the course of only a few weeks.

However, the biggest shock of all was when the new Royal couple announced to the press that as soon as was possible they were to marry. The King Conded the announcement by declaring quite rudely, "I'm expecting every single one of you peasants to turn up and cheer, but please could you make a bit more of an effort and not look as dismal and smelly as you usually do."

A ROYAL WEDDING WAS ALWAYS the nation's biggest and most joyful celebration. The capital would fill with thousands of loyal subjects who would line the streets twenty deep, cheering and waving to the Royal couple as they made their way through the city in a carriage.

People were given the day off, and the street parties always created a carnival atmosphere across the entire country.

But this Royal wedding day turned out to be very different from the ones of the past. As the King and his bride-to-be traveled from the palace to the cathedral, not a single soul turned up to cheer and wish them well.

The city was
completely deserted, except for a
chilling wind that whistled down the empty streets.

DAILY WORLD NEWS

THE KINGDOM THAT COULDNT CARE LESS !

ALL OVER THE WORLD the incredible story of the country that had chosen to ignore their own King's wedding became front-page news. Nothing like this had ever happened before, and journalists flew in from across the globe to cover the story.

The city was inundated with swarms of camera crews keen to hear the opinions of "everyday" people on the streets, who were unanimous in defending their defiance. They all agreed that as far as Royal families and kings were concerned, they had had enough!

Meanwhile, in the government offices, the Prime Minister called an emergency meeting to discuss this unprecedented turn of events. Backing up their findings with statistics and charts, the top ministers agreed that the political consequences of what had occurred should be taken very seriously indeed.

"According to our polls, Prime Minister," the most senior advisor summed up, "the general public are one hundred percent united on this issue, a statistic that has no precedent, and to go against such powerful popular sentiment could prove highly problematic for you and your party. I advise, sir, that you follow the crowd."

The Prime Minister was very aware that there was to be a general election at the end of the year. Appeasing the voters on this matter could be one way of assuring his re-election. If he supported the King now, he might be out of a job.

In Parliament the following morning, the Prime Minister stood up and made a passionate speech, declaring that the outdated tradition of a monarchy in this day and age was holding the country back: at a time when they should be advancing into the future, their once great nation was now an international laughing stock.

Everything that he said had been written for him by his advisors. Personally, he liked the Royal family; he thought they helped to keep people in their place.

After his speech a bill was proposed to dissolve the monarchy. None of the politicians wanted to be unpopular with the public and so it passed: the monarchy was no more.

As this astounding news traveled around the palace, Terry made his way to the office of Lord Von Dronus, who was packing his belongings. Terry looked him straight in the eye. "I think you should be aware that I know the truth about everything you have done," he said. The Lord's face suddenly went very pale. "But I'm happy," Terry continued, "to keep your secrets to myself on one condition."

Von Dronus opened his mouth as if to argue, but Terry carried on: "You have wronged two young people who didn't deserve it and I want you to put that right." And in a menacing tone, he added, "Or else!"

That evening the Lord appeared on television announcing that he was, due to the new circumstances, resigning as the Royal Protector. He went on to admit that in regard to the case of the two suspected enemies of the state he had been given incorrect information, and as such he offered his apologies to them and stated they were completely innocent and exonerated of all and any suspicion.

In a tall pink house on the other side of the city, Brian rose from his armchair and turned the television off. He smiled to his two young friends sitting on the sofa opposite as he said, "All of these recent events have been quite, quite incredible."

"Well, that's understandable," June replied as she looked at both John and Brian. "The world is an incredible place, full of incredible people."

ARLY THE NEXT MORNING,
John and June opened the front door
and stepped back into the outside world.

"This is what people do, isn't it?" John said
to June as they walked together to the park.

"Do what?" June replied, slightly confused.

John smiled as he looked across to her
and replied with just one word.

"Live."

They walked all
around the park, hardly
even talking, both of them
just happy to be there together,
in that moment, feeling a part
of the world again.

It was the time of year when the first
blossoms appear on the trees, and as lunchtime
approached people began to lay blankets down
on the grass.

"After we are dead, all of this will still carry on
without us," June said, thinking out loud.

"Yes," John agreed, "there will still be
picnics under the blossoming trees,
just as if we had never existed."

"And that's why we should never hide away from people
ever again," June continued, "because all we have
is time and it's too precious not to share."

FOR THE NEXT COUPLE of days they were very busy driving all over town, collecting and preparing food, so that June could start serving it to those who were hungry and lonely, just as she had done when John first met her.

When everything was finally ready, she drove her van to its usual spot and set up the folding table, laying out her pots of hot stew and bowls and plates and cutlery in readiness to feed anyone who was there.

At first the only people who came were a few individuals who were passing by, but within hours word had spread through the streets that June had returned and soon there was a line of people, including John's old friend, Big Jim. Even Brian came to lend them a hand, as well as Angelo and Theresa from the café where John used to work.

There were so many friendly faces, so happy to see John and June, that it seemed as if they had never been away.

Once everybody had been fed and everything packed away it was late and they were both absolutely exhausted.

They had just put their feet up when there was an unexpected knock at the door.

"I don't think I've got the energy to speak to anyone else tonight," June said, laughing. "Tell them to go away!"

But when John opened the front door, he could not believe his eyes. There, standing on the doorstep, was his oldest friend, the Bootman, and next to him John's mother.

Through all the hardships that John had endured since the night he left the palace for good, he had never shed a single tear in self-pity. He always saw each struggle as an obstacle to be endured until it could be overcome. He used to think that if he saw his hardships as friends rather than enemies then he could surely win them over. In his search to create a new life, it seemed as if there was an invisible force constantly pushing him forward, never allowing him to dwell on his own misfortune.

But now it seemed as if his strength had finally collapsed. He fell into his mum's arms as if he was once more not a prince or a king but just a small boy. And as he sobbed and sobbed he spluttered the words "Forgive me" through his tears.

"Forgive you?" his mother said as she kissed his head. "I'm so proud of you. You became the man you had to be."

OVER THE NEXT FEW weeks, John spent most of his time helping June to re-establish the food kitchen.

One evening, as June read her book and John sat drawing at the table, he looked up from his work and said to her, "I've been thinking. Would you mind if I stopped helping you? I've decided that I'd like to try to be an artist. This is what I feel I was born to do."

June smiled and said, "Of course. You must follow your heart."

The following day was a Sunday and John had arranged a surprise trip.

Since the monarchy had been disbanded, the Royal households had been opened up to the public so that everyone could enjoy the magnificent paintings and countless objects of great beauty.

John and June joined the long line of visitors and wandered through the ballrooms, dining rooms, and grand corridors with the rest of the tourists until finally, at the end of the tour, they came to a large stateroom where for a small fee you could dress up in the regalia of a monarch and have your photograph taken on the balcony.

"How about something to record this historic day?" John asked June.

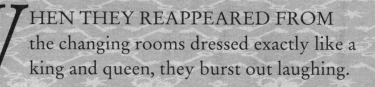

WHEN THEY REAPPEARED FROM the changing rooms dressed exactly like a king and queen, they burst out laughing.

The photographer positioned them on the balcony, saying to them as he focused his lens, "Very good. Now look at each other and can I have some lovely big smiles, please."

John took June's hand in his. "This is the real
beginning of my reign," he said, smiling shyly.
"Would you please be my Queen?"

Quietly, June said, "Yes."

"And can I be your King?"

June looked up and smiled at him. "You always were."

WELL, WHERE WE ARE, finally at the top of that mountain.

Phew! That was quite a climb!

I'm so glad that John and June made it to the top of their mountain.

Though it was hard work and at times they felt like giving up and heading back down, I'm glad they didn't because the view from where they are is breathtaking. It really was worth all the effort, and I hope they savor every moment.

And this is where we say goodbye to them.

And this is where I say goodbye to you.

Goodbye.

Libby
AND
Dave
22. VIII. 15

First American edition published in 2017 by
CROCODILE BOOKS
An imprint of Interlink Publishing Group, Inc.
46 Crosby Street, Northampton, Massachusetts 01060
www.interlinkbooks.com

Published in Great Britain by Hutchinson, Random House

Library of Congress Cataloging-in-Publication Data available

ISBN 978-1-56656-020-7

Text design by Carrdesignstudio.com

Mixed Sources
Product group from well-managed
forests and other controlled sources
www.fsc.org Cert no. TT-COC-2139
© 1996 Forest Stewardship Council
FSC

Printed and bound by Graphicom, Italy.

Huge thanks to the brilliant Jocasta "J-Lo" Hamilton,
the world's greatest editor.

Lots of love—The Robster